Hell is Empty

A Censored City Novelette

MELANIE HARDING-SHAW

ISBN: 978-0-473-51741-0

The author acknowledges the excerpt quoted from *The Tempest* by William Shakespeare, first published in 1623.

Publisher:
https://www.melaniehardingshaw.com/

CENSORED CITY NOVELETTES

Would She Be Gone

Compact of Fire

Hell is Empty

CONTENTS

CHAPTER 1

"Hell is Empty, Deanna? Seriously? Isn't that a little dramatic? That headline alone would alienate half our readers before they even get to the libellous content," Steve said.

"Of course, it's dramatic. It's Shakespeare! The Tempest. *Hell is empty, and all the devils are here*," Deanna protested.

She was standing opposite her editor in his office and she could hear the tapping of his stylus on his desk as he watched her. He was mad.

"It could be seen as blasphemy," he replied.

"What do you know about God? Grow a spine. Our readers don't care."

The stylus dropped to the floor. Steve's eyes narrowed and Deanna resisted the urge to clench her fists in response to his glare.

"Get out. Do your actual job. Leave this ridiculous obsession with Ganelon Corp alone. I already had to demote you. If you speak to me like that again, you're fired," he said, in a voice so low she had to strain to hear it.

Deanna opened her mouth to keep arguing and then thought better of it. Instead, she stalked from his office, ignoring the smirk of his personal assistant just outside the door. She'd not wanted to let Deanna in without an appointment in the first place. The woman was insufferable.

"How'd it go?" her ex-cameraman, Will, asked as she grabbed her bag from her desk, knocking over the potted cactus he'd given her for secret Santa the previous year "to match her personality".

Deanna looked over at him to see if he was being smug, too, but he just looked concerned.

"I'm not fired yet," she said.

"You need to just let this one go."

"They've obviously got senators and secretaries in their pockets. The media companies are no better, dancing to the tune of their advertising revenue. The Librarian was only ever supposed to censor limited mental health and crime triggers. It's completely out of control. They're just censoring whatever doesn't suit their profit margins. Someone has to call them out. I thought we were better than the rest of them, but we're just as bad."

Her voice was rising again and she fought to get it back under control before her editor heard and followed through on his threat.

"All you have is anonymous sources. You don't have any proof. You don't have anyone willing to go on record. What is he supposed to do?" Will reasoned.

"He could let me keep investigating. Let me do my job," Deanna snapped.

"Your job is reporting verifiable facts and producing enough words to justify your salary. It's been weeks," Will said.

His voice was calm. When they'd worked together filming news, he'd been the perfect foil for her dogged journalism. She had trusted him to know when backing off would get them a better story. But now she was running solo, demoted from the breaking-news livestream back to writing articles from bureaucratic press releases. And this time he was plain wrong, anyway.

She turned away and walked out the door before she said something she regretted. They'd worked together too long to ruin a friendship over this. But as she slung her bag over her shoulder and straddled her motorbike to head off to another spoon-fed press conference, she couldn't help but wonder for the hundredth time who at BT Media was being paid off by Ganelon. There was no question there would be someone, probably several someones. She really hoped it wasn't Will. Their friendship wouldn't survive that. And if it was her editor, she was royally screwed.

Her phone vibrated as she pulled her helmet on.

We need to talk. I want you to meet someone. 10pm at the safe house?

Deanna glanced up and down the street, and then told herself off for being paranoid. No one was close enough to be able to read her screen, and looking around like that would just make people suspicious. The number was programmed into her phone as "Contact 8C", anyway. Nobody would be able to figure out it was the fugitive, Virginia Wright.

Don't be late like last time. I need my beauty sleep, she replied.

She started the motor up and revved it hard, relishing the way the noise and vibration drowned out her thoughts as she pulled out onto the road.

Deanna reached the safe house early that night and settled in on the couch. Gini's coded knock on the door didn't come until quarter to eleven. Her head snapped up from where it had been drifting closer to her chest as she dozed. She cursed under her breath and rubbed the sleep from her eyes as she crossed the room.

She rapped out her own coded knock, all clear, and

then yanked the door open. She stood staring at the two women waiting outside. Or to be more precise, she stared at the woman standing next to Gini.

Deanna's head tilted to the side and one eyebrow rose as she looked the woman up and down. Her eyes tracing the unfamiliar sight of this particular woman in jeans and a baggy hooded sweatshirt that had obviously hidden her face for the trip here. She had loosened her black scarf and Deanna could just make out the hint of a bruise on her neck, revealed under make-up that had worn thin after a busy day in an office. Deanna had tried not to have any expectations of Gini after weeks of disappointment, but she definitely had not expected this.

"Ms Myers," the woman said curtly, nodding her head in greeting.

Deanna smiled, her eyes brightening as she sensed a crack in the walls that had been standing in the way of her investigation.

"Sera Olsen. Now this is a surprise. Come in."

"Play nicely, Dee," Gini warned, as Sera reacted to the predatory tone in her voice by starting to turn away.

Gini reached out to grab Sera's arm before she could walk off.

"We talked about this. We need her help," she muttered to Sera.

Deanna watched the interaction with interest, struggling to hide her amusement. Here was the woman who was personally responsible for writing Secretary Turnstin's appeals to the public for information on the fugitive cop Virginia Wright, apparently not only in contact with Gini but also willing to take her instruction.

Deanna moderated her tone and tried again. She needed whatever information this was about. "I'm sorry. I didn't mean to be rude. Please, do come in."

She watched Sera resist Gini's gentle pull for a moment and then her shoulders sagged and she stepped forward.

"Drink?" Deanna asked as she gestured for them to make themselves comfortable on the couch.

"Whiskey," Gini said.

"No, thank you," Sera added as she sat down on the single armchair, her body angled slightly away from the couches.

Deanna came back with three glasses of whiskey and put them down on the table, her smile daring Sera to say something.

"To unexpected visitors," she said, raising her glass to the two women.

Sera glared at her and then raised her glass in return, barely touching her lips to the amber liquid. She'd unzipped her hoodie in the warm apartment and Deanna was momentarily distracted by the way the soft light of her lamp played across the depression in between her collarbones as her chin lifted.

She forced herself to look away and caught Gini watching her with interest. Trust a cop to notice these things. She raised her eyebrows in a gesture of exaggerated innocence and took another sip of her own drink.

"So, what can I do for you? Tell your truth to the world? Write you an award-winning exposé?" she asked.

"This was a mistake," Sera said to Gini.

"Right now, we just want to talk. *Off* the record," Gini said.

"Of course you do," Deanna said, struggling to keep the sarcasm from her voice. Why go on record when you could make it the journalist's problem to run a story with no solid sources?

"Do you want to hear what she has to say or not?" Gini snapped.

Deanna sighed. "I want to hear what you have to say," she said, turning to Sera.

"Off the record? On your word?" Sera asked.

"Off the damn record. I swear."

She sat quietly as Sera explained the situation. It started off unsurprising. The Secretary for Literary Safety was being paid off by Ganelon Corp, just as she had suspected. They were messing with the Librarian algorithm to help the conservatives get re-elected. That wasn't unexpected either, but it was so brazen she was surprised no one had called them out on it already. By the time Gini was showing her photos of scientific reports that had been covered up and explaining that the author was now missing under suspicious circumstances, Deanna was sitting on the edge of her chair. She'd been right all along. Hell was empty and Ganelon Corp's devils were worse than even she had imagined.

Sera's usually clear voice dropped to a strained murmur as she continued. Deanna leaned forward to hear the story of the affair the Secretary for Literary Safety, Brenton Turnstin, had with the wife of Senator Bob McKay. Even cynical Deanna was shocked when she heard how Ganelon Corp had used their content algorithms to write seduction porn for him. It crossed a line from their usual blackmail to something much more sinister.

"The senator's wife, Grace, called me to ask for help. She wanted to stop the affair. Two days later she was 'overseas' and unable to be contacted. No one's seen her since," Sera said.

"Did you go to the police?" Deanna asked. There was no accusation in her voice, just curiosity.

"And say what? That the senator's office told me she's overseas, but I didn't know she was going? I have no proof. I even asked Senator McKay about her at a dinner function. He didn't bat an eyelid."

"Why did she come to you?" Deanna asked. She could always tell when someone was holding back.

"I run Brenton's office. I'm his fix-it lady. She knew that," Sera said.

Deanna watched her for signs of stress, but Sera had a good poker face. You couldn't front to the media every day without one. If she hadn't seen the love-bite on Sera's neck, she might not have connected the dots. But Sera's loyalty was legendary. It was common knowledge she didn't have a life outside of Secretary Turnstin's office, and certainly no time for a love life. She'd heard the rumours and put them down to sexist drivel. It was disappointing to find they weren't.

"Really? Or did she go to someone she knew had… first-hand experience with him?" Deanna asked.

Sera frowned and shoved herself to her feet. "This conversation is done."

Gini stood up and grabbed her arm. "Sit down, Sera. She needs to know everything or she won't be able to help us."

"What help are you expecting, exactly?" Deanna asked.

"I can't be seen in public and we can't risk Sera being discovered. My ex-partner Palmer's taken a job with the Feds. He can't risk that position. It took him months to find someone who'd take him on after they put him on leave for what happened. We need to keep the pressure on in the media and get the rumours of these missing people circulating, so he can convince his new boss to open a case," Gini said.

"Are you sure the Feds aren't compromised too?"

"No, I'm not sure. Palmer is looking into that."

Deanna observed the ex-cop for a long moment, her eyes narrowing before she forced herself to focus on getting the rest of the story from them. "So, what aren't you telling me? Other than that you're sleeping with the Secretary, which is obvious," Deanna asked Sera.

Sera scowled, but then collapsed back into her chair, defeated.

"We've always been... close. But now Ganelon Corp is using that to control me, with his blessing. Bren knows a lot about my family. He knows my sister has a mental health history. That's why I got into this business in the first place." Sera's voice became more strangled until it stopped working altogether and she sat staring at her hands.

Gini took over. "They've drugged her sister into a coma. She's lying in Saint Camillus as we speak. The doctors say she did it to herself, but she didn't."

"How do you know they're lying?" Deanna asked.

Sera spoke, her voice directed down at her open palms as if the words were blood pooling there, staining her conscience. "Because Riley's never taken a pill she didn't have to in her life. I was pushing back too hard on Ganelon's activities in our office. Bren thinks he can use my sister to manipulate me back into wanting to help them."

"So, call him out on it," Deanna said, her voice sharper than she intended. She couldn't stand it when women did nothing to save themselves.

"Sera is pretending to believe him so she can help us bring them all down. At considerable risk to herself, I might add," Gini said, the steel in her voice telling Deanna she needed to back off.

"Your testimony alone could take the Secretary down," Deanna said.

"But he would be replaced by someone just as compromised and they would use him as the fall guy. They'd make it all his fault and the Librarian algorithm and the arrests would carry on as if nothing had happened. We need to take the whole system down, not just that one man," Gini said.

"So, let me check that I understand. You want me to publish articles about the people disappearing, but you won't speak up in support and I have to keep all of this evidence you've brought me completely *off* the record just in case it leads back to you?" Deanna asked. She could feel the anger boiling up inside her.

"Yes."

"You're as bad as she is, Gini. Neither of you gave a shit about this stuff, about the truth, until it affected you personally. You were quite happy arresting people until it was your own family being arrested. She was quite happy propping up a corrupt system until it hurt her sister. No one is going to publish this without a known source and corroboration. I'm not throwing my career, and possibly my life, away so that you two can salvage your consciences in the way that is most convenient to you. It could take years to get a federal investigation completed. The only reason not to go public now is to protect yourselves. Come back to me when you're serious about making a difference. I'm out," Deanna said.

"You have no idea what you're talking about or how many people in the resistance movement put themselves at risk. Every. Single. Day. To break this corruption open. You only see the tip of the iceberg," Gini's voice was low and clipped, her face unreadable.

Somewhere during her rant, Deanna had shoved herself to her feet to leave. She wanted to run this story so badly it hurt, but they weren't really interested in exposing anything. They just wanted to use her as a distraction. That was the kind of attitude that let these corrupt people keep popping up like damn cockroaches. And it was the kind of attitude that left a journalist arrested, homeless and hungry, or dead.

Will had been right, she needed to let this one go.

CHAPTER 2

All of the next week, the conversation with Gini and Sera replayed in Deanna's mind. Should she just try and get Steve to run it anyway? Publishing the missing person allegations would be too far without proof. But surely even Steve wouldn't turn his nose up at leaked science reports no matter what he'd told her about dropping the investigation.

She was still pondering the question over breakfast on Thursday when her phone rang. She'd been idly toying with the idea of going undercover at Ganelon, but she hadn't got further than staring vacantly at her stash of surveillance equipment before realising everyone there would know her face from the news.

It wasn't like the early days of her career when she'd built a reputation from exposing the darkness hidden in plain sight around them. Her mentor had been a paranoid burnt-out ex-cop and she'd spent two years learning everything she knew about breaking in and out of systems and buildings. She'd also been left with a lasting appreciation for whiskey, self-defence, and leverage.

She shook herself out of her memories and checked her caller ID, wincing when she saw it was Steve. What did he want now? He hadn't spoken to her since their argument.

"Deanna? Justin's called in sick and Laura's an hour's drive away. I need you to front the livestream of the first day of hearings of the commission of inquiry with Will. You're the only one available with enough background to run with it this close. Don't give me any of your attitude though. Just facts. Can you do it?" Steve's voice was urgent, but clear. You had to be calm under pressure in a job like that.

She checked her watch. She had about twenty minutes to get fifteen minutes across town.

"Sure, I can do it," she said.

"I'm serious, Deanna. Give me any shit and you're done here."

"I get it! Roses only."

She hung up and scrambled to get changed into something suitable for the camera. As she was running out the door, she paused by the table and scooped up a spy-cam. She might not be able to get one into

Ganelon, but there was no reason she couldn't get her own personal feed going from the inquiry. Maybe she could learn something from the closed sessions.

Will was already set up at the entrance to the building when she arrived.

"We've got three minutes to film an intro before Senator McKay gives his speech," he said in greeting.

Deanna took in his hunched shoulders and tousled hair as she dropped her bag by his feet and stepped in front of the camera. He must have been called up last minute as well. Will was all about the prep and post-production. He was the guy who always wanted one more take, just in case. This was not his kind of rodeo.

"Ready," she said.

Will straightened his posture and turned the camera to her, and then paused. "You're going to behave, right?"

"Two minutes," she said in reply.

He swore under his breath and the red filming light came on the camera.

Deanna stared down the barrel of the dark lens. It had been a while. The familiar calm descended, extinguishing the adrenalin buzz that had carried her here. She was barely aware of the crush of other journalists around them, the smells of coffee and anxiety that permeated the steps to the inquiry building.

"We're coming to you live from the first day of hearings on the commission of inquiry into the literary safety system. The inquiry's chair, Senator Bob McKay, will give an opening statement shortly. The Secretary for Literary Safety announced the inquiry in response to the mass protests that arose after revelations of large-scale censorship by the Librarian algorithm and the Agency for Literary Safety. The key suspect in revealing the censorship, Virginia Wright, is still at large. The Secretary has already come under fire for his appointment of a chair many consider incapable, and for the narrow terms of reference that focus only on the recent breach of the literary safety system and specifically exclude whether that system is operating as intended. We're crossing to the inquiry chair, Senator McKay, now."

Deanna timed her delivery perfectly. She could tell when she needed to wrap up without needing to look by the sudden drop in the noise around her. She deftly stepped out of shot, allowing Will to zoom in on the senator just as he reached the podium.

She tuned out as the senator gave his opening address. There would be no opportunity for questions and she doubted anyone around her would have let her get one in anyway. She watched him leaning forward, lapping up the attention. Explaining it was his "honour" to serve as chair. He didn't look like a man whose wife was captive or worse. And that made him far more dangerous than she had given him credit for.

When he'd finished speaking, they all filed in behind him to film the first session. There was a brief and silent jostling for position as they each tried to get the best angle. Deanna braced herself to hold the space around Will as he set up.

"Really, Dee? The Secretary has 'already come under fire'? Only from you! Stop pushing!" Will hissed.

Deanna grinned at him and turned her face back to the front of the room. She had felt her phone vibrate in her pocket three times already. She wasn't going to check it, though. If Steve was going to tell her off, it could wait until later.

As silence fell once again, Deanna shuffled sideways to lean against the wall. It was one of those overly ostentatious rooms designed to make anyone giving evidence understand exactly how insignificant they were.

The commission members were half a step higher than everyone else, with their large cushioned seats. Everyone giving evidence was packed together on hard wooden seats with the press breathing down their necks behind them. The room had high arched ceilings that made your voice lost without a microphone that's volume was tightly controlled. The press area was standing room only, another obvious power play given the long hours these hearings usually ran for.

The walls were decorated in intricate carvings, relics of symbolism from another time that still served as the exclamation point on the end of the room's statement: I house power! The carvings were also a convenient place to casually slip a spy-cam into the shadowed ridges of the carved robes that made up a depiction of Justice. The undulating shape let her position the lens in exactly the direction it needed to go.

The opening session was barely an hour, more for show than anything else. The chief executive of the Agency for Literary Safety listed statistic after statistic of all the things they'd done right and no one in the commission seemed inclined to question too deeply. Deanna rolled her eyes in disgust. She hoped they did better in the closed sessions without the media. What a joke!

They paused on the way out of the building to record a concluding segment for their piece.

"Day one saw the whitewash begin as—"

Will let the camera dip and his voice cut over the top of her "Give it a rest, Dee! Stick to the basics and you might not lose your job. Try again."

Deanna glared at him. "Don't you care about what they're doing?"

"Yeah, I do. But I care about paying the rent, too."

"They are hurting people!"

"And when you get a credible source, on the record, I will absolutely back you up with Steve. Until then, stop trying to get us fired!"

Deanna looked away, staring down the street at the drab-coloured bureaucrats hunting out lunch and coffee, bodies subconsciously leaning into the sunshine before returning to their ant holes. Everyone dutifully not getting fired, she assumed.

She looked back at Will. He looked genuinely concerned about her. It was written in the lines stretching from pleading eyes, the hand hovering uncertainly by his side because he knew she didn't want him to reach out. Stop trying to get *us* fired. She owed him that much, at least.

"Fine. Let's get this over with," she relented.

She checked her phone on the way back to the office. Three texts from Steve:

What did I say about sticking to facts?!

The Secretary's office has banned you from the press room.

You're on community stories for the rest of the year.

Deanna swore to herself. She was too good to be stuck reporting kids' sport and local fairs. Damn him. And so much for Sera wanting her help. Everyone knew Sera ruled the Secretary's office. Why the hell had she banned her from the press room?

"Did you get fired yet?" Will asked.

"Worse," Deanna replied.

"You only have yourself to blame."

19

"That's really helpful, Will. Thanks."

They finished editing the story, minus her comments about the Secretary, by the end of the day. Deanna reviewed what was coming up tomorrow and winced—a tree planting and a story about a playgroup in a retirement home. Screw that.

She stormed across the office and ignored Steve's personal assistant's protestations as she slammed his door open.

"Can I help you?" he asked. His head was pointedly tilting towards the guest in his office, a ginger-haired young man in a suit jacket and black jeans that screamed 'tech'.

Deanna looked closer at him, her eyes narrowing as she noticed several readers visible in the gap of his briefcase leaning against the chair. Not many people had more than one. Was he from Ganelon? What was he doing meeting with Steve?

She did a quick adjustment. No way was she giving anything away to this guy.

"Sorry, had to catch you before I head off. I'm going to take some holiday leave," she said.

"Can we discuss this tomorrow?"

"I'm taking leave tomorrow."

Steve paused and looked at his guest again. His stylus tapped a single time in agitation, not enough for anyone who didn't know him well to pick up on his annoyance. Deanna hoped she hadn't pushed him too far.

"Fine. You could use a break. Send through the details before you go."

"Thanks. I'll do it now."

She got her phone out as if she was starting an email. She managed to swipe the camera on as she turned around and sneaked a photo of Steve's guest as she walked back towards the door.

That night, she flicked the photo to Gini in a text.

Any idea who this guy is?

The response came an hour later.

Sera says it's the Ganelon liaison in the Secretary's office. Where did you see him?

In my boss's office after Sera banned me from their press room.

She says she didn't have a choice, Gini replied.

Bullshit. What are you two doing, anyway?

Jealous? She's not my type. Talk to her yourself. Take her for a drink. It sounds like you could use one.

Deanna swore as she saw Sera's contact details pop up on her screen. *Screw you*, she wrote back.

You're not my type, either.

CHAPTER 3

It took three hours for Deanna to run out of things to clean in her apartment the next morning. What had she been thinking? She should have just gone to the damn tree planting. Or maybe not. The towel under her window was soaked from the rain leaking through. The only thing more miserable than community news, was community news in the rain.

She collapsed on her couch and grabbed her reader. It had been forever since she'd read something for fun. And maybe she could check out those stories that Sera had talked about. The ones designed to get the conservatives re-elected. Nominations were heating up as they neared the primaries. She would have been right in the thick of it if she'd kept her mouth shut on Ganelon.

She sighed and looked at the clock. Was it too early for a drink? Maybe conservative lit wasn't the way to go. She scrolled through the new releases and picked one at random, a thriller of some sort. She read an excerpt:

Anna Myer could hear her floorboards creak as she cowered under her desk. In the darkness, she could just make out the sharp thorns of her cactus impaling the carpet where it had fallen to the floor. She'd known she was messing with the wrong people, but she just wouldn't back off. She'd always worried that if she came out, her life would be over. Now it really would be. There was only one thing to do—destroy the evidence before they destroyed her.

Deanna threw the reader away from her. Those Ganelon bastards. Did they think they could threaten her into staying silent? Or that they knew anything at all about how "out" she was? She crossed the room and stomped on the plastic and glass until she heard the already cracked screen shatter under her foot.

There was no way she was letting this go now. She set up her laptop on the table and connected to the spy-cam feed from the inquiry. While she waited, she pored over the reports Gini had sent her.

She read about the increasing severity of mental health incidents from the very people the Librarian was supposed to help. People who had already felt ostracised and isolated before the Government took away their right to access the ideas and words that everyone else could.

Even the crime stats were going the wrong way, partly because of the crackdown on literary safety crimes and partly because, if anything, permanent censorship restrictions on criminals seemed to increase the reoffending rates. The exact opposite of why the algorithm had been developed in the first place.

And then there were the disappearances that she was just as unable to turn up any evidence of as Gini and Sera. The chief medical officer that had gone missing seemed to have no family to complain, and if Senator McKay had noticed his wife had dropped off the face of the earth, he was showing no signs of it.

The audio on her laptop crackled to life as the inquiry got back underway. Deanna shut down her other searches and pulled up the feed. The angle wasn't great, but the sound was OK if she turned it right up. They were questioning the chief of police.

She leaned back in her chair and closed her eyes to focus on the audio. The chief described the night that Virginia Wright snuck into the Cybercrime headquarters and downloaded a virus into the literary safety search system that shut down all censorship restrictions for 80 percent of readers in the area. They still hadn't resolved the problem. Gini had told her the virus was designed by a disgruntled Ganelon programmer. She would have loved to meet her. Dee smirked as she listened to the chief describing Gini's "unstable personality".

The chair led the questioning with the usual patsy questions: "How had the breach affected their ability to protect the community? Were they seeing an increase in violent incidents?"

Dee leaned forward at the table again as the other commission members finally got a word in.

"Was a risk assessment of the search system undertaken? Why was it rushed out into the field only days after the new legislation passed?"

Dee opened her eyes to try and see who had asked the question.

"The priority was getting the content and biometric monitoring underway, so we could save lives as soon as possible."

"How many lives have you saved with biometric monitoring through people's readers, Chief Hale?"

Dee grinned as she recognised the clear young voice. Alex Treyn was the most liberal appointee to the commission. Likely only appointed as they ticked so many diversity boxes in a single seat. That was a miscalculation on the chair's part. Alex wasn't known for making public statements, but they were sharp as anything and relentless.

"That question is out of scope, commissioner," the chair rebuked. The chief hadn't even started to respond. He must have been briefed beforehand.

"I'll rephrase. How many searches of content and biometric data have you run since the new law came in?"

"We run hundreds every day."

"And how many of those would previously have required a warrant?"

"I don't have the figures available."

"You're an experienced officer. Guess."

"I don't have the figures available."

"OK. Let's try some different information. How many arrests have been made by the Cybercrimes Unit for literary solicitation in the last calendar year?"

"327."

"Whose role would it be to check that the censorship—sorry, the 'literary safety restrictions'—of a particular reader that had been breached in those cases was justifiable under the law?"

"The solicitation law is clear. It states you cannot solicit material that has been restricted from your reader. The programming and quality assurance of the Librarian algorithm by Ganelon is completely separate and irrelevant to those prosecutions."

"Commissioner, this line of questioning has veered out of scope again. Why don't you let someone more experienced continue?"

"I disagree. This commission was set up in response to public concerns that the scope of censorship had exceeded the intention of the law. The question of who checks that and how is directly relevant."

"The purpose of this commission is to establish what caused the breach of the literary safety system," the Chair corrected.

"And isn't it likely that the breach arose from a valid concern by citizens that the Librarian algorithm has exceeded its intended use?"

"Let's take this off-line and resume tomorrow."

Dee heard Alex objecting, but it was muffled by the noises of rustling clothing and rising conversation as the rest of the commission stood to leave.

She turned the computer off and sat staring at her own dim reflection in the dark screen. Alex wasn't sitting around waiting for an investigation. They were fighting on regardless, from the inside. She might not be able to do anything with Gini and Sera's "off the record" evidence, but that wasn't the only information she had. She'd been gathering stories of people who had been hurt by the literary safety system for months. Steve wouldn't publish them, but she sure as hell could present them to this commission. Maybe she could shame them into growing a backbone before they questioned Ganelon.

She turned the computer back on and found the online form to register to give evidence to the inquiry. Before she could rethink, she filled in her details.

She spent the rest of the week gathering her evidence together. Interview transcripts, statistical analyses of Ganelon's content trends, the raw data behind the science reports she wasn't allowed to release. Anything that might tip a wavering commissioner into scepticism.

Despite all of that, she wasn't really convinced the inquiry would let her speak. When the invitation came through for a date the following week, she stared at it blankly. Maybe Ganelon's fingers weren't everywhere after all, or maybe they just wanted to find out how much she knew. Either way, she wasn't going to back out now.

She knew Gini would flip when she heard though. This wasn't part of her grand plan. Deanna didn't fancy one of her late-night visits through her fire escape when the fugitive found out, so she flicked her a message.

Presenting to the inquiry next week. Don't worry, I won't mention you or Sera.

What good will that do? Don't make yourself a bigger target than you already are, Gini replied.

Deanna turned her phone off.

CHAPTER 4

On the Tuesday night before she was due to speak to the commission of inquiry, Deanna stood practising what she was going to say in her bathroom mirror. It wasn't something she'd done since her first months as a livestream journalist, but this felt different.

She looked down at her notes for the third time and frowned. She'd never had so much difficulty keeping the structure of a statement in her mind. Should she emphasise hard facts or personal stories? Worst cases or the far more numerous and insidious everyday effects?

She heard her phone vibrating on the kitchen table in the other room. She glanced at her watch. It was after 11pm, whoever it was could wait. She shifted her feet apart and straightened her posture, which had wilted with each extra minute she spent practising. But as she opened her mouth to carry on, the noise of her phone interrupted her again.

She swore and stalked into the dining room to snatch it off the table. Unknown number. She thought about letting it go to voicemail, but now she was curious. She'd barely put it to her ear before Sera's urgent words cut through her annoyance.

"Deanna, get out of your apartment! Someone's coming."

"Sera? What are you talking about? Who's coming?"

"I'll explain later. Right now, you need to leave! Please!"

Deanna had already grabbed her jacket. There was something in Sera's voice that instinctively set her moving, a strained undernote of genuine fear.

She was reaching for her front door handle with the phone tucked under her ear when it smashed inwards toward her, sending her crashing to the floor.

Pain flared in her wrist and hip. Two masked figures appeared in the doorway. She froze for a split second. They weren't expecting her to be on the floor right there. A steel-capped black boot lurched forward, carried by the momentum of the body that had broken down her door. It was a hand's width from her sprawled legs.

Deanna levered her body up and kicked hard at the knee closest to her. She didn't wait to see the results, she was already scrambling to her feet and shoving her hall table towards the black-clad men as she ran towards the kitchen. A hand wrenched at her shoulder as she fled, but the table slowed him down.

Her eyes scanned the bench for anything she could use. She grabbed a whiskey bottle and twisted to hurl it behind her. She heard a curse as it bounced off an attacker's arm before smashing on the ground between them.

That space between them was too small. She backed away, hearing the crunch of broken glass underneath their boots as they approached more carefully. They knew she had nowhere to run to. Her hand reached out blindly for the knife block and came away with a paring knife. The others were all in the sink.

She fought to keep her panic under control as she watched the men draw closer. They had batons in hand now. Not here to kill her then. At least that was something. She held the tiny knife out in front of her. Her hand was shaking, but it could still stab one of these bastards before they took her down.

They stopped three paces away, one slightly behind the other and off to the side. The one in front hung his baton back on his belt and held his arms palm out.

"Our employer just wants to talk. No one needs to get hurt," he said, his voice muffled by the black balaclava that covered his mouth. He lifted a foot to step closer.

"Don't!" Deanna shouted. She had meant to sound forceful, but even she could hear the pleading in her voice.

He paused.

She breathed in deeply and tried again. Calm. In control. "If your employer just wants to speak with me, they can arrange a meeting like anyone else."

She was stalling, but her whirling thoughts weren't coming up with any ideas for getting out of this. And as the adrenaline spike of the initial break-in settled down, all that was left was fear. She didn't even notice her hand with the paring knife lowering to her side, subconsciously accepting defeat.

"You can tell them that when you see them," he replied, stepping closer.

His punch came out of nowhere. His fist, intended to catch her under the jaw, pounding into her cheekbone instead when she flinched away. She raised her hands to ward him off, the forgotten paring knife catching on his sleeve. The tiny nick was enough to slow him down, but only long enough to grab her wrist in vice-like fingers and squeeze until she could no longer grasp the handle and it clattered to the floor.

She shut her eyes, not wanting to see the next blow before it came. Her swollen, throbbing cheek was launching tears streaming down her cheeks.

She heard a thump and a male voice cry out. The other attacker. The sound of a baton smashing against a cupboard jerked her eyes back open. She had just enough time to process the fact that there was a third figure in the room before a gunshot rang out. The noise felt like a physical blow to Deanna's already stunned and aching brain.

Through the ringing in her head, she heard a man cry out "Pull back!"

The guy holding her shoved her to the ground. Pain radiated up her spine from her tail-bone as she fell backwards and by the time she looked up, all she could see of the attackers was a flash of movement around the corner as they made a quick retreat. Deanna tried to make her eyes focus on the person still standing in her kitchen who seemed poised to chase the men but then looked down at her and sighed instead.

"I told you not to make a target of yourself. We need to get you somewhere safe," Gini said.

Deanna let Gini pull her to her feet and tongued at her teeth as she led her to the door. She could taste the metallic tang of blood where the inside of her cheek had been cut, but the teeth themselves still seemed to be firmly attached.

Gini took her down the corridor to the fire escape at the other end of the floor and out the window. Deanna was still in too much shock to protest and before she knew it they were clattering down the swaying old metal ladders clinging to the back wall of the apartment complex.

There was a silver car waiting in the alleyway and Gini bundled her into the backseat as soon as her feet made contact with the tarseal.

"Hi, I'm Jonas," a man said from the front.

Deanna stared blankly at him for a minute and then belatedly introduced herself. "Deanna."

"Drop her at Sera's for now. We can figure out something else tomorrow," Gini said.

"What? I'm not hiding because of those bullies!" Deanna said, her brain finally kicking back into gear.

"We can talk about it tomorrow. It's late. You need somewhere safe to crash, and you can't stay with us."

They sat in silence for the rest of the drive.

Gini walked Deanna all the way to Sera's door and then left her waiting for it to open. After the way their last conversation had ended, Deanna wasn't sure what to expect.

Sera opened the door in flannelette pyjama pants and a singlet, but that wasn't what caught Deanna's attention, at least not for long. It was the look of intense relief on her face. The frantic eyes searching her face and body for signs of injury.

"You're OK," she said, more to herself than Deanna.

"Not the most glowing praise, but I'll take that as a win from you," Deanna said.

"Shut up."

As Deanna stepped through the doorway, she was caught by surprise as Sera pulled her into a tight hug.

"I thought you were going to be Grace all over again. Or my sister," Sera whispered into her shoulder.

Deanna hugged her back awkwardly, and then pulled away. She could still smell the scent of vanilla from Sera's hair. Her voice turning over-bright as she made herself focus on the pillow and blanket stacked neatly on the minimalist white couch in the living room.

"Still here, and not in a coma. Unless you're a figment of my subconscious," she reassured.

"You can sleep on the couch. I'll get an icepack for that," Sera said, reaching out to touch the bruise that was swelling on her cheek.

Deanna froze in place until she'd turned towards the kitchen. She should have flinched away from that touch, but all she'd wanted to do was turn her face into it. It must be the shock, she told herself. Or the head trauma. But she'd had a concussion before and she was pretty sure she didn't have it now. Sera had always been an opponent to spar with, a gatekeeper to push out of the way. Her traitor body needed to get a grip.

"Here," Sera said, returning with an icepack and two glasses of whiskey.

"I didn't think you drank."

"Only on special occasions," she said, the corner of her mouth twitching upwards as she settled next to her on the couch.

Deanna held her crystal glass up to clink with her. "To special occasions."

They sat in silence on the couch. The fiery drink drove the last of the numbness that Deanna had been feeling away.

"So, do I need to worry about Secretary Turnstin showing up in the middle of the night?" Deanna asked.

She regretted the question as soon as she asked it. Sera had been staring into the distance and now her eyes tightened and looked away.

"Sorry. That wasn't fair," she added.

Sera met her gaze with a look of surprise at the apology. How awful did she think she was? It was Deanna's turn to look away.

"He's out of town. I don't know how much longer I can keep up this charade," she said. Deanna could hear the defeat in her voice, the self-loathing that was creeping in.

"I don't know how you do it. I can pretend to like the most annoying politician I'm interviewing, but my lovers always know exactly how I feel." Her eyes flicked down to Sera's lips before she looked away again.

"I have a responsibility to try and fix this. I do it because I don't have any choice."

Deanna swallowed the words she wanted to say—there's always a choice. Sera's choice had probably saved her life tonight.

"Thank you," she said, instead.

That drew a small smile out of Sera, as if the win of saving Deanna was a piece of wreckage she could cling to in the stormy ocean that was this shit-show.

"I'm going to try and get some sleep," she said and she reached out to squeeze Dee's hand.

They sat like that for longer than they should have and Dee wondered where the boundary was between a reassuring gesture and holding hands. She held herself perfectly still, not wanting to break the moment. Not wanting to scare her off. It was Sera who sighed and drew her hand away in the end. Dee tried not to read anything into the way her fingers trailed along her palm.

"Thank you," she said again, as Sera stood to leave.

And then she turned away to start laying out the blanket on the bed. She didn't trust herself to hold back if they kept talking. Whatever that moment had been, it was a complication she didn't need in the middle of everything. Especially with a woman who had enmired herself in a self-destructive relationship with a narcissist and now couldn't leave.

She watched Sera pause from the corner of her eye and then she heard her footsteps as she made her way across the wooden floor to the bedroom.

CHAPTER 5

Deanna couldn't sleep after everything that had happened. The white leather couch made noises every time she turned over to find a more comfortable position. The oven clock was making a soft buzzing sound that she wasn't sure how to stop. The room was two or three degrees warmer than she would ever have kept her own bedroom, just enough that the blanket was too hot, but throwing it off was too cold. Plus, it left her feeling exposed in the strange apartment with someone who was only a little more than a stranger to her sleeping in the next room.

A little after 5am, she gave up. She left a note for Sera and quietly let herself out.

She couldn't face her apartment on her own. The door had been broken when the men burst in. Anyone could be waiting there. Instead, she slipped in the side entrance to her office and showered there. She always had a change of clothes in her lower desk drawer, just in case.

It wasn't until she looked down at the cactus on her desk with her hair still dripping that she remembered the story on her reader. She resisted the urge to dive under her desk, but her hands shook as she grabbed her things and ran for the stairs. She left out the basement garage exit, her eyes searching the dim artificial light for any sign of movement, her ears straining to catch a sound of anyone hiding in the shadows.

Sunlight was barely brushing the tops of the gargoyles looming on the rooftop over the entrance to the inquiry building when she arrived. It wouldn't open for another two hours. She wished she could have stayed in her office.

Deanna sat with her back to the memorial wall in the park across the road, staring at the double doors at the top of the entry stairs. She pulled a muesli bar from her pocket and chewed it methodically, wishing she'd thought to grab a cup of coffee.

As natural light filtered back into the world around her and drove some of the night's spectres away, her head started lolling backwards against the cold stone. She forced herself to stand and read the headlines on her phone to keep herself awake.

Immigration and crime top issues for Senate hopefuls

Ganelon Corporation launches mental health charity

"A reader saved my son." Mother credits new parental alert function with saving son's life

Deanna couldn't keep the scowl off her face as she scrolled down in search of any genuine journalism. The protests had shrunk to almost nothing while the public awaited the results of the inquiry. She couldn't blame people for biding their time. They still needed to earn a living. But the inquiry itself should still be major news, even without thousands in the streets.

The first mention of the inquiry was page two of results, an opinion piece by a Senate candidate— *Literary Safety Inquiry the latest in a string of wasteful spending.* Just another political football to score points from.

When the doors opened at 8am, she gratefully left the exposed park for the shelter of the waiting room for the inquiry. They were starting at nine and she was the first due to give evidence.

She sat on the hard, wooden seats and resisted the urge to pick at the nail heads that studded the hand-crafted chairs, leaving painful dimples across her legs.

At 9:45, the commissioners passed by her on their way to the inquiry. At 10:05, the red-haired man who had been in Steve's office the other day held a whispered conversation with the receptionist, and then made his way down the corridor to join the commissioners.

"Excuse me," she called to the receptionist.

"Yes?"

"Is there some delay?"

"Ganelon needed to give some more evidence. You'll be on once they've finished," the receptionist explained.

Gini texted mid-morning: *Everything OK last night?*

Yes.

Have you come to your senses yet?

I'm sitting in the inquiry reception now.

I thought Sera would talk you out of it.

She didn't bother dignifying that with a response.

Lunchtime came and went.

Deanna fumed in her seat. If they thought she was the type to give up just because of a wait, they didn't know who they were dealing with. You didn't get to be an award-winning journalist without the ability to stick at a story.

The red-haired man emerged mid-afternoon.

"I'll take you through now," the receptionist said.

Deanna's head started up from where it had sunk to her chest and she blinked her eyes to focus them, just in time to catch the man smirk and give her a little wave. She resisted the urge to make a rude gesture.

The inquiry room seemed a lot bigger without the crowds of media she was used to, but the walk from the doorway to the witness seat passed too quickly. Deanna fought to gather her scattered thoughts together, glad she had taken the time to practise even if her brain kept trying to drag her forwards from the memory of speaking at her bathroom mirror to the sound of her door crashing in.

"Commissioners. Thank you for the opportunity to speak to you today—"

"—One moment Ms Myers. Before you start, could you clarify what expertise or direct involvement you have that justifies your right to present here," the Chair interrupted.

"I—"

"—The Commission accepted her request. We've already wasted most of a day in tedious and irrelevant testimony. She's here. Let's get on with it," Commissioner Alex Treyn cut in.

Deanna sat schooling her face to careful blankness as the inquiry commissioners argued the point another twenty minutes before she was allowed to start.

"Proceed," the Chair said, waving a hand at her without looking and then picking up his reader to inspect a document before she had even started talking.

"In my online submission, you can see the data presented clearly. It is based on publicly obtainable information and clearly shows the statistics that politicians and the media have been at pains to twist into a different story—"

"—or perhaps it is you who are twisting it, Ms Myers," the Chair interjected.

Deanna carried on, speaking over the top of him, "Hospitalisations and treatment for acute mental health conditions have plummeted since the Librarian restrictions were brought in, but talk to any decent medical professional and they will tell you, with a straight face, that beta-blockers are useful as a treatment for a sprained ankle or asthma or any number of other routine conditions that have seen a commensurate sharp increase. They know their patients won't seek help if they face the stigma of 'safety' restrictions.

Aggravated assault arrests have halved, but there is no data on the volume of assault complaints and at the same time literary safety arrests have increased tenfold. The drop in assault arrests is not a benefit of literary safety restrictions, they're a side effect of police resources being redirected. And if you look at—"

"—Thank you for your *theories*, Ms Myers. That's all we have time for. We have your written submission," the Chair said, pushing himself to his feet.

Four of the other commissioners immediately followed suit, leaving Alex Treyn and one other looking on in annoyance.

"You kept me waiting for six hours and then tell me you're out of time?!" Deanna called after the Chair's departing back. He didn't even turn around.

She blinked in confusion at the sun as she stormed out of the building. There was no natural light in the depths of bureaucracy and the day had already been so long that she was sure it should be night time. She couldn't face public transport, so she just kept charging on down the sidewalk barely noticing the people who took one look at her face and stepped out of her way.

It wasn't until she was staring at her splintered doorframe that she remembered why the day had been so long in the first place. She froze in place with her hand poised to push the door open. There was a sticky note from her neighbour underneath the door's security peephole.

I hope everything's OK, Dee. I heard the floorboards creaking last night outside the door. Did you mess with the wrong people again?

—R

She took a step backwards, and then another, as if the door itself might jump towards her and attack. Rachel had moved in a year ago, two doors further down the hallway. They'd even had a brief fling over Christmas that they'd both agreed to pretend hadn't happened in the interests of neighbourly boundaries. There was no way the wording of that note was co-incidence. It was the same as the story on her reader. Ganelon was everywhere, and they wanted her on the run.

She walked slowly with her head held high until she reached the stairs, then she tore down them as quickly as she could, trying not to overthink the soft echo of her footsteps ricocheting of the walls. It was too late to stop her from giving evidence. They just wanted her to back off. No one was following her. Probably.

She ensconced herself in a café with bottomless coffee eight blocks away and texted Sera.

Sorry to bail this morning. Any chance I can crash on your couch again tonight?

After two hours, her eyes were aching from the effort of staying open and she had to admit Sera wasn't going to reply. Maybe she was regretting whatever connection had started between them the night before.

She stumbled her way through two bus connections to the safe house where she had first met them. She had no idea if it would be occupied. She couldn't face dealing with Gini to ask.

No one answered her knock on the door and the lights were off when she entered the apartment. It felt like the weight of the world was hanging off her arm, pulling her to the ground as she bolted the door behind her. By the time she'd checked every corner and cupboard for an attacker, her feet were shuffling, barely lifting off the floor. She didn't even bother pulling her shoes off before collapsing on the bed.

It was mid-afternoon when she was woken by her phone.

"What?" she growled.

"Have you heard from Sera?" Gini asked.

Deanna sat upright as a shot of adrenaline coursed through her.

"Not since the night before last. Why?"

"She was supposed to meet me at lunch. She didn't show."

"Maybe something came up."

"She would have messaged. She knows how risky it is for me to meet. We were trying to sort a cover for how we had been tipped off to the attack."

Deanna swore. She'd been so caught up in her own problems she hadn't even thought about how Sera had found out she would be attacked and the danger that put her in. Her unanswered text suddenly seemed more ominous.

"I don't want to put her in more danger by searching her apartment if it's nothing, though," Gini said.

"Leave it with me for an hour," Deanna said.

"You can't be seen there either."

"I won't be."

Her first call was to Will. Fingers crossed in front of her that he wasn't being paid off by Ganelon as well.

"Dee? What's up?"

"Did you cover the Secretary's press conference today?"

"Yeah. Why? I thought you were on holiday."

"I'm getting bored and I heard a rumour. Who from his office was supporting him?"

Will sounded intrigued. "That new press advisor. Hamish, or Hadleigh, or whatever his name is."

"Thanks!"

She hung up on his questions and ignored her phone when he called back. Where else would she be? She tapped the phone on the arm of the couch as she thought back to the conversation they had in this same living room. She remembered Sera's broken voice as she talked about her sister Riley in the hospital.

She put the phone back up to her ear and dialled Saint Camillus. "Hello. This is Mrs Olsen, Riley's mother. My daughter Sera's lost her phone and I can't remember when I was supposed to be meeting her there. Have you seen her lately?"

"Mrs Olsen! Great timing. I haven't seen your Sera, but we were just about to call you to tell you Riley's brain activity is up. It's early days, but it looks like she's finally coming out of it!"

Deanna stabbed her finger to her screen to hang up, hoping they'd think she'd been cut off and call the real Mrs Olsen back. She felt sick with guilt at having stolen that news from Sera's family. Then her brain kicked back into gear. Ganelon had been drugging

48

Riley to keep control of Sera. If Riley was coming out of it, they must have stopped. They didn't need to control Sera anymore.

She dialled Gini's number, oblivious to her tears running down the glass of her phone where it was pressed tight to her face. "They've got her. What do we do?"

CHAPTER 6

Deanna stared around the basement headquarters of Gini's resistance movement, impressed despite herself. She'd known Gini had been busy, but she hadn't quite expected the tables of high-power computers lining the room's walls, or the number of people engrossed in whatever it was those machines were being used for.

A wiry, grey-haired man was doing something in what looked like the back end of the story network that the Government readers accessed. Next to him, a young woman who couldn't be more than eighteen was typing code so fast the cursor on her screen couldn't keep up.

Gini pushed her gently towards the glass table in the middle. The driver from the other night, Jonas, was sitting there poring over the map of the city displayed across the table's surface.

She recognised the man next to him as Cameron Palmer, Gini's old police partner who had lost his job when she hacked the cybercrimes network to spread the reader virus. She remembered Gini saying he was working for the feds now. She hoped Gini hadn't misplaced her trust in him. He could just as easily be investigating them undercover, in which case she had just secured herself a trip to jail by being seen there.

She leaned forward over the table to peer more closely at the map, careful not to touch the surface so it didn't mess up the display. A handful of buildings glowed blue against the otherwise monochrome display. She knew at least three of them were Ganelon facilities, those were all marked with grey crosses. Gini saw where she was looking.

"Those marks are too obvious. They're the first place the police would search if they ever got the balls to get a warrant against Ganelon. Too risky to hide anyone there."

"Assuming they're hiding her at all. If she's a threat, they'd be better off eliminating her," Palmer said from across the table.

"They'll want to find out what she knows about us," Jonas replied.

Deanna blanched at Palmer's blunt assessment. "Then we need to find her now."

"Sera mentioned she found records of a domestic airport they own under a shell company just out of town. We sent someone by a month or so back to investigate. Security there was pretty tight, and we didn't know what we were looking for so we just left someone watching it. I think that's our best bet," Gini said, zooming in on a bright blue area on the far side of the table.

"What are we waiting for, then?" Deanna said.

Gini and Palmer shared a look. "There's a big difference between hacking a network and storming a secure facility. We don't have that kind of firepower," he said, in the kind of patient voice you use with a slow child.

"What would it take to get the Feds in there?" Deanna asked. Her mind felt clearer than it had for days. Sera needed help. That was all she needed to focus on. She'd saved her life and she owed her this.

"The evidence Gini and Jonas have collected got me permission to investigate. There have been enough internal investigations shut down at Cybercrimes to raise a few eyebrows. It's just a matter of figuring out who we can trust. My boss might show her hand if there's a big enough public problem," he said.

"What are you thinking?" Gini said, sounding wary.

"Cameras. Livestream as soon as we find something. Get the footage to enough devices so there's no way to cover it up. Can you do it?"

The teen at the nearby computer spoke up. "It's all we can do to keep ahead of them as it is. With a livestream broadcasting from here, they'd find us before you got anywhere."

"What if I can get you into BT Media's news channels?"

The teen grinned. "Now we're talking."

"They will know it was you. You'll be a fugitive," Gini said softly.

"You and Sera saved my life," Deanna said.

"Body cameras aren't going to protect you from a bullet," Palmer pointed out.

"But if they can get past the outer security, and we feed Ganelon and the media the footage once they're inside, then they will know they can't just shoot them without a public outcry," Jonas replied.

"If you feed Ganelon the footage, they will know exactly where to find us," Gini said

"They'd find it anyway. It's just a matter of whether they find it before or after they shoot you."

"This is a terrible plan," Palmer groaned.

"Sera could be being tortured or shifted to another country as we speak," Deanna said.

Gini swore under her breath. "Alright let's do it. No guns on our side. Don't give them any more excuse than they already have to shoot us."

Jonas reached down to his ankle and unclipped a sheath hidden underneath his pants. He tucked the knife into Gini's hands and kissed her hard. Deanna looked away.

"How do we get in?" Gini asked

Jonas gestured to a thin red line running across the width of the runway. "We mapped the security camera fields when we did the original recon. We knew we might need to get in there at some point, so our team managed to install some kinetic street art a month ago. It will help screen your approach on this side. You can park down this side street, approach through the art, and then use the bike tunnel underneath the runway. One of the cameras on the other side was knocked a little off centre and there is a black spot there where you could cut through the fence."

"Why aren't there any cameras in the underpass itself?" Deanna asked.

"It's a public road, not Ganelon's property. The cameras are all on their perimeter fencing," Gini said.

"And they've been known to use the tunnel as a black spot for their security guys to rough up unwelcome visitors," Jonas muttered, then he looked up at the women beside him and half-smiled reassuringly, "but they won't send anyone there unless they suspect something or an alarm triggers."

Deanna blanched and went back to peering at the map, trying to get a sense of scale.

"That black spot by the fence isn't any wider than me!" Gini said, staring at the area next to the fence they would have to cut through.

"The perfect size," Jonas said, but his eyes betrayed his concern.

"Looks like it was made for us. Let's do it," Deanna said, ignoring the fear that threatened to overwhelm her.

Gini met her eyes for a long moment and then nodded. "We won't get a better opportunity. As soon as they notice that camera needs adjusting, we're screwed. Let's do it."

"I need to go talk to my boss. She won't want to discuss this on the phone," Palmer said, shoving himself away from the table.

Deanna watched him go. Her thoughts were reeling. She remembered the night Gini had told her she was only seeing the tip of the iceberg of the resistance movement. She'd been right. The people in this room were impressive enough, but how many groups were in the field right now putting themselves at risk to lay the foundation for nights like this one? She shook her head in amazement and went to sort out camera options and access to BT's network with the teen.

"I'm Skye," the teen introduced herself, "So, what's the plan for BT's system?"

"An old and very cantankerous colleague taught me to always keep some leverage because you never know when you might be left high and dry," Dee explained, "I set up back-door access to the livestream channel after my boss arranged a meeting with me to discuss my 'performance'. Good thing I did, too, because he demoted me to text media the next day."

Skye moved aside and let Deanna take over the keyboard, her eyes following every keystroke closely.

"It's a little basic, but I think I can make it work," she said when Deanna had finished.

Deanna frowned at the little upstart and muttered something about ungrateful youths of today under her breath.

Skye laughed. "I mean, you're probably old enough to remember paper. Was there still newsprint around when you started?" she teased.

Deanna shook her head and opened her mouth to retort that she was not THAT old, you little... but Gini's voice cut across them.

"Ready to go?" she called.

"No. But let's do it anyway," Deanna replied.

Skye reached out and squeezed her hand as she stood up to leave. "Good luck."

Gini was silent in the car as they headed out towards the airport. Deanna's mind spun through a list of worst-case scenarios and which of her friends and associates might be compromised. Was everyone who'd tried to pick her up in the last year a Ganelon agent? What else did her neighbour know about her that would put them at risk? Did it even matter after she burned all her bridges on this scheme?

Gini's voice broke across the low hum of the motor. "You'll need to turn your phone off and just use the burner. We don't want to make it any easier to find us."

Deanna pulled out her phone and saw she'd missed a bunch of texts from Will.

—I know you're chasing down a lead. I'm not even going to tell you to stop. Things have been getting weird since you went on leave.

—I meant what I said the other day. If you've got a credible source, I'm behind you all the way.

—Dee? Are you OK?

She looked over at Gini. There was no point asking her what to do. She'd say not to trust him. But Deanna's gut was saying Will had her back just like he always had.

I'm going offline for a little bit. Why don't you see if there's anything useful in here—she attached a link to the storage of the live feed from the inquiry. She hadn't had time to trawl through it. If everything blew up in her face maybe Will could still get some gems from there. She switched the phone off before he could reply.

Dee shifted in her seat and adjusted the body camera where the seatbelt was pushing it against her chest.

"When do we start recording?" she asked.

"There's a sign for the airport near the street art our people installed. If we get both in shot it will be harder to claim we've staged it."

The buildings passing the car windows were turning more industrial as they reached the fringes of the city. Apartments and corner stores gave way to car yards and warehouses. The car pulled in next to a wire-link fence.

"We'll approach on foot from here," Gini said, opening the door.

Deanna felt her fear start to turn into the thrill of chasing a story. She stood tall next to the car as Gini strung pouches onto her belt and tucked tools from the trunk of the car into them. She watched the streetlight reflect off the steel of a small bolt cutter for the fence. She had no clue what the other packages were.

Gini lowered the trunk gently and pushed it closed with the softest of clicks, not that Dee could see much point when they were standing on an otherwise empty street exposed to any cameras by the street lights and the security lights shining out from the entrance of the adjacent monolithic corrugated-steel building that followed on from the fence they were parked next to.

"All set?" Deanna asked.

"I feel naked without a firearm." Gini reflexively smoothed down her jacket over the pouches she had just filled

"Welcome to how the rest of us function all the time," Deanna said, her voice harsher than she meant it to be, more accusing.

Gini just glanced at her and then set off down the street.

"I didn't mean it like that," Dee said as she caught up. She remembered the sound of Gini's gunshot in the kitchen. The power it had held to make those men run away, a power her shaking hand holding a kitchen knife had lacked.

Gini shrugged. "I know. People deal with stress in different ways." She looked over and must have seen something of Deanna's guilt in her face because she reached out and clasped her arm. "Don't worry about it."

The two women reached the street corner side by side and Gini held her arm out to stop Deanna from stepping past the cover of the building they were flanking. She kept her body screened by the building and leaned her head forward just enough to get eyes on the way forward.

"It's clear. But keep close to this building as you approach so the sculptures can screen us," she said.

Deanna followed her as she edged around the corner. As she cleared the building, she could see a short stretch of cul-de-sac ahead of them. Beyond Gini's silhouette immediately before her, she could make out dark shapes like saplings at the end of the stretch of road. They were waving in the breeze that was tugging at her hair and lit from below by spotlights that cast an eerie blue-green light upwards.

As they drew closer, she saw they were some kind of kinetic, layered, wind sculpture. The long structures created a chaotically mesmerising pattern as each one shifted on a different axis. She couldn't see through the lights and shifting shapes to the fence beyond, but she could imagine the glint of the spotlights on the security camera lens she knew was facing this way. Months of surveillance by Gini's resistance friends had mapped their fields of vision.

She was so busy watching ahead that she didn't notice Gini hold up a hand to stop where the building finished beside them. She stopped inches from her back, close enough that her hair brushed across her face.

"Cameras on. We'll need to speed up from here," Gini whispered, gesturing to the sign across the short gap in front of them—*West Erten Airfield Underpass*.

Deanna took a breath and connected her burner phone to the camera to start the livestream. She couldn't help but feel like she'd started a countdown to an explosive. It was only a matter of time before Ganelon would find them. Everything hinged on them finding Sera before that happened.

Gini raised an eyebrow at Deanna and stood to the side so she had a clear shot. She had a camera too, but Deanna was the professional. Hers was just a back-up, an insurance measure.

Deanna whispered down to the camera's microphone. They had agreed to keep names out of it at this stage, in case they found someone they weren't expecting.

"This is Deanna Myers, live from the outskirts of West Erten Airfield, a cargo-plane facility owned by a series of shell companies that can be traced back to Ganelon Corporation. We are unarmed. We have reliable information that at least one person is being held against their will in this facility. We are going to attempt to enter and find them. To reiterate, we are unarmed. We are not a safety risk to anyone in the facility. The video feed will stream as long as we are able."

She nodded to Gini that she was ready to go.

"Follow my lead," Gini hissed, pulling down clear glasses that should help her track the path of the red lights that would be flashing underneath each security camera. It would help them identify any cameras they might not have identified, and check their vision fields hadn't shifted too far. It wasn't foolproof, but it was better than nothing.

She watched as Gini stooped down low and ran across the gap to the wind sculptures, and then followed suit, careful to tilt the camera on her chest upwards so whoever was viewing online could see more than just the shadowy concrete and her boots.

The two women kept close to the rustling metal poles as they skirted around them and then commando crawled across the remaining gap towards the underpass, a steep ramp leading down under the runway.

Deanna had been in some tight spots as an investigative journalist, but she had never felt quite so exposed as she did crawling headfirst down those two body-lengths of rough concrete path under the night sky. There was nothing to hide behind except the ethereal gap between the top of her hair and where they hoped the camera's view stopped immediately above them. Every breath of wind felt like the sweep of sinister eyes watching them draw closer to the dark tunnel where anything could be waiting.

Gini reached the shadow of the tunnel's entrance and drew the knife Jonas had given her from her boot, holding it tight to her thigh out of sight of Deanna's body camera.

Deanna reached the tunnel entrance and leaned her back against the cool sides where there was still some light from the artwork, massaging her hands that were stinging from the loose stones she had pulled her body over to get there.

"We need to keep going," Gini said, shining her cellphone torch into the darkness and taking off at a jog without looking back.

Deanna dragged herself to her feet and followed after. The only thing worse than being attacked in a dark tunnel was being attacked alone in a dark tunnel. She ran to catch up and reached out to hold Gini's shoulder as they jogged. Deanna was out of breath by the time she could make out the dim light at the other end, but they both sped up in unspoken agreement.

Compared to the commando crawling, pushing their chests up hard against the concrete wall to the tunnel and the security fence on the other side was easy. But their shuffling sideways steps made Deanna feel like they were edging along a narrow mountain path with a plummeting drop beyond the edge of their heels. At least once they reached the fence she could grasp her fingers through the metal wires to keep herself steady.

She clung there with her cheek pressed up hard against the fence as she watched Gini carefully extract the bolt cutters from her pouch and set to work. She was sure the marks of the diamond shape of the metal would be pressed into her skin for days.

She watched Gini's hands shaking with effort as she clamped the nose of the cutters around the wires. They were not much bigger than pliers to keep them out of the camera's field of vision, and as sharp as they were it still took a lot of hand-strength to cut through the thick fencing. As the first snap of success sounded, Deanna realised she'd forgotten about the camera she was wearing, and she reached up to point it towards Gini's activity.

Deanna couldn't help but be impressed as the small woman methodically made her way up the links of fencing—snap, snap, snap. When she reached the top, she shook her hands out for a minute before carrying on along the top. Then she peeled back a section of fence just big enough for them to contort themselves through.

When they were through to the other side, they stood staring across dry grass and the runway towards the complex of buildings on the other side.

"What now?" Deanna asked.

Gini held a finger over the microphone on her camera and Deanna did the same.

"That was as far as our intel takes us. We're on our own from here. Now we run," she said.

Deanna swallowed hard and forced herself to think of Sera instead of every other instinct in her body that was telling her to get back through that hole in the fence before Ganelon found them.

Instead, she took her finger off the microphone and took a step forward through grass that crunched under her feet.

"We have made it into the complex. We've probably only got minutes until we're found. If you're watching from home, wish us luck."

Then the two women took off at a run, feet pounding underneath them as Gini pointed to the end of the building that was furthest from the entry. Furthest from where the guards would likely be stationed.

There were fewer lights here, just the dim light from the entrance to the complex ahead and to their left, and from a handful of windows in the main airport buildings. The night was clear enough that they could even see stars above them. It would have been beautiful if Deanna had been able to focus on anything but searching the shadows ahead of them for movement. Skye would have waited until they started running to send the feed through to Ganelon, if they hadn't already stumbled across it. The building was looming above them when they heard the first shouts off to their left.

"Shit," Gini said, even though they'd both expected it.

The hangar door was closed, but there was a small entrance door to the right. They sprinted towards it and Gini slammed her shoulder into the door, falling through it with a cry when she realised it wasn't actually locked.

"I guess they were relying on their security cameras," Deanna said, reaching down to haul the other woman back to her feet where she had sprawled on the ground.

Gini spun past her and slammed the door shut behind them, locking it with the deadbolts that had been left unlocked before.

"Let's go. That won't delay them for long," she said.

They turned back into the hangar and ran underneath the nose of the looming aircraft towards the rest of the complex.

The door ahead of them sprang open towards them as they reached it and Deanna barely had time to register someone was coming through before Gini had sidestepped and kneed them hard in the stomach. She slammed the hilt of her knife down onto the back of his neck as he grunted and doubled over. Stepping over him to check the corridor for any more.

"Come on," she hissed to Deanna, who was still staring at the black lump of clothing lying on the ground.

Deanna shook her head and stepped forwards, grabbing the man's firearm to unload it as she passed before throwing the now harmless weapon into a pile of crates nearby.

"You know your way around a firearm," Gini whispered in surprise.

Deanna smiled grimly. "Not just a pretty face," she said, pushing past Gini into the passageway to the main airport complex.

"Don't get cocky," Gini hissed to her back.

CHAPTER 7

Thankfully, the corridor between the buildings was short because there was nowhere to hide. It emerged into a warehouse full of wall-to-wall shelving stacked with boxes. Deanna scanned the words on the sides of them with the light from her phone—government e-readers.

That was interesting in itself because Ganelon wasn't supposed to have any input into the hardware side of the system, one of several "fail-safes" to prevent corruption or a monopoly. So much for that. The shelf above was full of boxes labelled 'emo.nitor'. What the hell was that?

She was reaching out to try and open a box when Gini grabbed her phone out of her hands sending them into darkness. She felt the woman's calloused finger press against her lips and then heard the sound of soft footsteps from the other side of the warehouse a split second later. Gini shoved her down to the ground behind the bottom row of boxes just as the overhead lights flickered on, leaving them blinking in the bright light and exposed to whoever would come looking.

Deanna risked poking her head up above a box to try and get a look at how many there were. She pulled her body camera up as well, it was high res and there was a chance someone watching would be able to zoom in and identify the people approaching. As she ducked back down again, she heard a strangled cry from the passageway beyond that was cut off as the door shut—"Help!"

"Sera!" she yelled out without thinking, and the sound of footsteps turned into the clomping of boots running towards them.

Gini swore and dragged her to her feet to circle around the far side of the shelves. They dove through a gap in the boxes, sending a handful crashing to the floor to block the way. One row closer to the door and Sera. Then another.

Deanna was so focussed on pushing through before the men reached them that she didn't notice Gini's absence until a voice called out "Stop!"

Her head jerked up and she watched a man coming down the row towards her, stepping around the mess of boxes that had tumbled to the ground. She could see the movement of black fabric on the other side of the hole she had been making through the boxes. She couldn't dive through and escape.

She turned to the man and stood straight, making sure her camera was pointed straight at him. He was pointing a Taser at her, his feet slowing as he approached. She had just enough time to take that in, and then a box crashed down on his head from above with a sickening crack. His body crumpled to the ground. Deanna glanced up and saw Gini jumping from the top of one shelf to the next. She didn't wait to see who else might appear, she ran straight past the collapsed form, stooping to grab his Taser from his limp hand, and out into the main central corridor. She tore towards the door, the memory of Sera's cry drawing her on.

Gini caught up to her as she neared the door. She spun towards the flicker of black clothing in her peripheral vision, adrenaline surging.

"I almost shot you," Deanna hissed.

Gini grabbed the Taser off her and carried on. They were almost at the door when Gini jerked back and then dove towards the left. Deanna ran forward just in time to see her body stiffen and collapse, the copper wires running from her body to the Taser in her attacker's hand reflecting in the harsh fluorescent overhead lights. Deanna knew a fair amount about Tasers from her early exposés on police brutality.

A distant part of her mind noted how close Gini had been when the Taser had fired, how her body had twisted. It wasn't a clean hit. It was enough to give her hope her friend might pull through in time to help.

The attacker had to keep hold of the Taser and couldn't move or he'd risk snapping the copper wires. Deanna tucked her head down and tackled him low, grabbing for the Taser at the same time. She couldn't wrestle it from his grip, but it was enough to snap the wires.

And then she was sprawled on top of the muscled and angry security guard. What the hell had she been thinking? She tried to throw herself backwards, her hands scrabbling for anything she could use as a weapon. His sweeping forearm threw her even further, and pain exploded through her back as she hit the metal shelves behind her.

She barely had time to register that hit before she was being grabbed by the lapels and hauled to her feet. The man's face was expressionless as she met his eyes for a terrifying moment. Then she flinched instinctively as his forehead crashed towards her face. The headbutt cracked into her cheekbone instead of her nose. Years of self-defence classes finally kicked in and she slammed a fist towards his groin. When he twisted away she grabbed a handful of inner thigh instead and twisted hard. As soon as he loosened his grip to deal with that, she threw herself sideways and away, just in time to see the two points of Gini's Taser slam into his chest and his body stiffen.

"You OK?" Gini called.

Deanna looked over and saw she was still sitting on the floor, leaning semi-prone on one of the boxes.

"Yeah. I think so."

"My legs aren't working right yet and I need to keep this guy out of action. You keep going."

Deanna nodded and dragged herself to her feet, waiting for the world to stop spinning before staggering towards the woman.

"What about you?"

"I'll stun him and follow. I'll be fine in a couple of minutes. Go get her."

Deanna reached down to clasp her shoulder and then shoved the door open and stepped through.

She walked down a long corridor that must have been white at some point, but was now cracked and grey. The faded brown linoleum was stained in patches that could have been water leaks or could have been something more sinister. She glanced through an open door as she passed and saw a single bed bolted to the floor and a toilet in the corner.

Deanna forced her tired legs to speed up, careening down the corridor. They had a head start and they were moving Sera. She wouldn't get another chance. She reached another door like the one she'd entered by and paused with her hand on the bar that would push it open, catching her breath. Then she shoved it wide and dove through it to the side, hoping she wasn't about to be shot.

She landed behind some sort of aircraft loading buggy and peered around it at two Jeeps sitting with their lights on. The garage door was open. She was almost too late. She peered at the one closest to her and saw someone sitting in the back seat guarding something, guarding some*one*. She just hoped that someone was Sera.

She crawled into the driver's seat of the buggy, keeping her head low and hoping they didn't notice the movement. She didn't know what they were waiting for, but she couldn't waste the opportunity. Her gaze swept across the unfamiliar controls and then she pressed what she hoped was the starter and slammed her foot down on the accelerator. She'd meant to park it in front of the Jeep she thought Sera was in and block them in, but she misjudged the broad turning radius of the vehicle and instead she slammed into the side of the Jeep sending it pivoting sideways to land jammed hard against the buggy facing the wall.

Her neck ached with the impact and her sternum smashed into the steering wheel before she was thrown out of the buggy all together on the wrong side from the Jeep. She tried to stand, but her body was starting to give out on her.

Her vision was blurring, but she could just make out shadowy figures running to the other Jeep. Her heart sank as she heard the squeal of tyres accelerating out of the garage.

"Sera!" she cried out.

She heard a groan from the other side of the buggy. A groan from a woman.

"Sera?"

Deanna hauled herself upright and staggered around the buggy towards the stationary Jeep. Both doors were open on the far side and she peered inside the backseat. She was rewarded by Sera's face staring back. She was handcuffed to a bolt in the floor.

She had just enough time to climb in the back and wrap her arms around Sera before she heard the engines of multiple vehicles tearing into the garage. They were all out of options. Sera clung to her hand with knuckles turning white.

The armed woman who pointed her firearm into the backseat was just another black-clothed threat. Deanna stared down the barrel of the weapon and waited for oblivion. It took her a moment to process what she was saying.

"I'm a federal officer. Stay put while we clear the building."

Deanna could feel Sera shaking in her arms and pulled her body even closer. The next intrusion into their space was a camera lens. A familiar friend for her, but she felt the body she was holding stiffen and try to push backwards. She moved in front of Sera, screening her from the camera's view as she got out and stood bracing herself against the car.

Now that she had more space, she could see the cameraman—Will. He winked at her as he adjusted his position so she was in shot. She sighed in relief and straightened her posture as much as she could.

"Ms Myers, the world has been watching your livestream footage. Can you tell us what happened here? Where is your partner? Who did you find?"

"When we arrived, the Ganelon security staff were clearing the facility. There are one or more cells in the adjacent building for holding people against their will. The woman behind me was abducted and held captive for saving me from their men, who attacked me in my own home."

Will's camera swung around to a federal officer returning from the way Deanna had come.

"Assistant Director, what did you find?"

The woman frowned in annoyance and then smoothed her face out as the camera swung her way.

"The facility has been emptied. We found one deceased body. We will make a statement when we've had a chance to debrief."

Will put the camera down as Deanna slumped against the door. "Who is it? Who died?" she called to the woman as Will placed a hand under her elbow to brace her.

An officer approached with bolt cutters and gently shifted her out of the way to set to work on Sera's restraints.

"We'll have to get an ID and notify the family before we can say," the woman answered.

Deanna watched as two officers carried a body bag from the corridor she had entered from, towards the waiting cars. One of them slipped on a patch of oil.

"Careful! Don't drop her," the other said.

Deanna blanched and resisted the urge to tear the bag open and see if it was Gini.

"Dee?" Sera croaked from behind her, she was standing now, rubbing her wrists where the restraints had left deep red welts.

Deanna hugged her tight again. Sera turned her face towards her and rested her head on her chest before turning towards Will's voice.

"Come on, ladies. Let's get you to the hospital," he said.

Without even really speaking about it, Deanna went home with Sera after the hospital and stayed. The text from Gini came within hours of the police and media storming the airport—*I got out fine. See you around.*

Deanna respected Sera's grief and kept out of the media storm that their rescue had incited. Will had texted a cryptic message early on and for once she took his advice—*Maybe don't read the news until you're feeling better.*

Instead, she disconnected from the world to sit and talk with the woman who had once been her adversary and was quickly becoming much more. They curled up on the couch under a blanket and listened to music. They brushed hands making coffee in the morning and smiled.

She spent days holding Sera in her arms as she sobbed with guilt when the Feds called to tell them the dead woman had been Grace, the missing wife of Senator McKay. She'd been shot when Ganelon's people had realised the facility had been breached. She must have known too much.

A week after the night of the rescue, Deanna climbed quietly out of bed and left Sera sleeping to go check the headlines. She couldn't disconnect forever. She needed to know. Her swearing when she read was loud enough to wake her new lover.

Secretary for Literary Safety arrested for abduction and imprisonment of lovers, including Senator's wife

Her eyes traced down the words of the story, fuming. According to the article, Ganelon had rented the building where Sera had been held to Secretary

Brenton Turnstin. Ganelon was going to get away with everything.

Sera came to read over her shoulder. "Shit. They found another fall-guy. I told Bren he was stupid to trust them. He got what he deserved."

"It's not all bad," Deanna pointed to the next heading—*Literary Safety programme halted indefinitely.*

"At least we managed something. The boxes in the warehouse and the inquiry hearings will be enough to bury the programme for good," Sera said.

Deanna put the reader down and stood to wrap her arms around Sera. "How do you feel about the programme shutting down?"

"It never should have been set up in the first place. Did I tell you my sister is going to run for office? I've agreed to be her political advisor."

Deanna raised her eyebrows. "That's brave of her. Brave of you."

"It's necessary. Nothing will change if we don't get rid of Ganelon's puppets. They're already talking about using those emo.nitors to track prisoner's emotions and predict reoffending when they're released. It's only a matter of time before we're right back where we started."

"Need a media advisor?" Dee asked.

Sera grinned and kissed her. "I was hoping you'd say that."

Dee smiled. Maybe hell was still empty and the city was still full of Ganelon's devils, but they weren't invulnerable. No more reporting from the sideline. This time she was joining the fight.

Enjoy what you read? Please leave a review!

You can subscribe to Melanie's newsletter at:
www.MelanieHardingShaw.com

ABOUT THE AUTHOR

Melanie Harding-Shaw is a speculative fiction writer, policy geek, and mother-of-three from Wellington, New Zealand. Her short fiction has appeared in publications like Daily Science Fiction and The Arcanist, and she was a finalist for Best Short Story in the 2019 Sir Julius Vogel Awards.

You can find her at:
www.MelanieHardingShaw.com
Facebook @MelanieHardingShawWriter
Twitter @MelHardingShaw